Toulouse on the Loose!

Toulouse on the Loose!

Oh, Toulouse, where are you going, mon ami?

Written by Kimberly Thompson

Illustrated by Chris Easey

Little Pigeon Books
Downers Grove, Illinois

Toulouse on the Loose!
Written by Kimberly Thompson
Illustrated by Chris Easey

Copyright ©2009 by Kimberly Thompson

First printing 2009
Second printing 2011

ISBN: 9780981897622
LCCN: 2009930567

Manufactured By:
BookMasters, Inc.
30 Amberwood Parkway
Ashland, OH 44805

Date Manufactured: April, 2011

Job #: M8361

Dedication

I dedicate this book to my Creator, the best storyteller I know.
To my late grandparents, Carl and Blythe Schultz from Buffalo, New
York, and Fort Erie, Ontario, who could spin an earthly yarn that
would simply enchant their listeners for hours.
To my family and friends for their encouragement and
unfailing support through this whole process, and to
all my students, some of my greatest teachers.
And to you reader, for beginning this journey with me
and for exploring the world of Toulouse,
a foreigner's life here on this planet.

This book belongs to:

_____

Author's Notes

Our characters soar beyond words. Toulouse, the turkey, and his guide, the Pigeon, find themselves on a quest for freedom. Coming from the Moulin Rouge, in Paris, and making their way to the District of Columbia, they discover together how Thanksgiving became a national holiday in the United States of America, and how the truth sets one free.

Thanksgiving has a long history, beginning with the Pilgrims in 1621 and their friends, the Indians. Together both parties had a three-day feast in honor of harvest, friendship, and survival of the harsh winter. This event was based on Succoth in the Old Testament during ancient biblical times.

Later in the 1700's, our first President, George Washington, asked the citizens of the thirteen original colonies to set aside a day for thanksgiving. At this time, there was not a unified day. Each family could celebrate how and when they wanted to.

However, this changed during our country's Civil War during 1861 to 1865. President Abraham Lincoln requested a national holiday to count our blessings even in the midst of a torn apart north and south. This day was to be symbolic of preserving the Union. In addition to proclaiming this annual event, the president also pardoned the first turkey at the White House. The Lincolns were given a live turkey as a present for their Christmas dinner. Tad, their son, asked if his father would pardon the turkey like so many of the prisoners of war were set free. Sure enough, Mr. Lincoln obliged and the turkey became a favorite family White House pet. This act of kindness eventually developed into the annual pardoning of the turkey at the Rose Garden.

As for the Thanksgiving date always being on the fourth Thursday of the month of November, President Franklin Delano Roosevelt was responsible for this task.

OUR CAST OF CHARACTERS
The Pigeon in ancient Greek represents dove, a symbol of greater peace.
Toulouse, the turkey, is based on the famous artist, Toulouse Lautrec, who spent time at the Moulin Rouge in Paris where he studied his craft.

Toulouse,
is on
the loose.

Ready for
a "la Trek."

Planning
to visit
the USA,

two weeks
before Thanksgiving Day!

Little did he know,
during November snow…

turkeys in
America

aren't just
the Stars
of the show!

Our French feathered friend
takes to the sky,
as we are reminded

only wild turkeys
can fly.

And so,
    being quite debonair,
    he decides to take
        "French Air."

Our artist desires to paint
all the Landmarks of
the states.

Beginning with the
Nation's Capitol and

ending with the
Golden Gates

Flying into B.W.I.

He decides to give a train a try.

It rambles on to D.C.

where he hails down a...

Taxi!

The driver spies Toulouse on the curb,
instinctively
thinking of
spices and herb.

Toulouse gets in
and makes a request,

"I hear L'Enfant Plaza's bakery is the best."

Stopping at a familiar site,
Toulouse thinks, *Ahhh!* A baguette
with seeds, greens and berries
will taste just right!

Relaxing at the
pâtisserie,

the *boucher*
next door, is
waiting to implore.

28

"Ooh la la! Come into my kitchen for some fine food preparation!"

31

Our reluctant
friend retorts,

"*Non merci*, I think not.
I'm here to do the turkey trot."

First stop
is the Mall.

Toulouse will
have a
Ball!

With an artistic tool in claw,
Toulouse sets up and begins to draw.

Seeing the great
memorials ahead,
"Magnifique" is
what he said.

While Toulouse makes his
final embellishments,
a tiny pigeon gives her compliments.

"Sir, you have made
some masterpieces,
but before you can make more,
you must first understand
our country's historic
score.

"When America was
at civil war ...

the 16th president addressed the congress floor.
Mr. Lincoln made an official proclamation,
uniting the country in national celebration."

Toulouse interrupts,
"Say, all good
Frenchmen love
a soirée."

"Setting aside," pigeon continues,
"a day to count our blessings
complete
with roasted
turkey and all
the fancy
dressings."

Toulouse starts huffing, "*Excusez moi!*
You mean with cccccranberry stuffing?"

Pigeon replies,
"*Oui!* I hear
it is quite a
jubilee!"

Our
tourist friend
protests,

"That shall not be my fate!
I will not end up on anybody's dinner plate!

Pigeon responds,
"I know this much is true.
The president pardons
one turkey a year
and that bird
could be
YOU!

I just hope
it's not
too late!

We must hurry to the White House gate!"

I'll cross the reflecting pool...

Whoops!

Oh, dear...
he's done it
again.

Not frozen
yet...hee
hee

lifted into the air.

Pigeon squawks, "Hey, you're flying!
You must be wild!
or at least a little riled!"

"*Oui*, I guess I just forgot.
So long, I've done my turkey trot.
Pigeon encourages, "Oh do not worry.
Now we'll get there in a hurry!"

Thus they flew, without further ado,
over Constitution Avenue.

From above, they plainly see,
a grand White House in full ceremony.

They make a turn, land with grace,
and end up in a rosy place.

Awed by the pair's arrival,
the President ponders
our friend's survival.

"A Pardon? For me? Oh! Mr. President .... Im ..... so ...... happy, ..."

He decides to give this
foreign bird a break,

with a certificate of pardon
and a presidential handshake.

And...
a hug.

Gratefully,
Toulouse goes on his way
after wishing everyone a very

FREE and...

HAPPY THANKSGIVING DAY!

Our heroic friend goes down memory lane...
while his little companion hopes there was...
wisdom to gain!

Where will Toulouse
   go next?

Here is a clue...

"Give me your tired, your poor,
Your huddled masses yearning to breathe free,
The wretched refuse of your teeming shore,
Send these, the homeless, tempest tossed to me,
I lift my lamp beside the golden door!"

—Emma Lazarus, 1883

Glossary

Baguette—A long, rod-shaped loaf of bread

Boucher—Butcher

Cuisine—Food

Debonair—A refined manner

Enfant—Child

Excusez moi—Excuse me

Jubilee—A season or occasion for joyful celebration

Magnifique—Magnificent, splendid

Merci—Thank you

Merci beaucoup—Thank you very much

Oui—Yes

Pâtisserie—Bakery

Soirée—An evening party or reception

Recipes

Toulouse's Favorite Cranberry Bread

2 cups sifted all-purpose flour

1 cup sugar

1 $\frac{1}{2}$ teaspoons baking powder

1 teaspoon salt

$\frac{1}{2}$ teaspoon baking soda

$\frac{1}{4}$ cup butter

1 egg, beaten

1 teaspoon grated orange peel

$\frac{3}{4}$ cup orange juice

1 $\frac{1}{2}$ cups light raisins

1 $\frac{1}{2}$ cups fresh or frozen cranberries, chopped

Sift flour, sugar, baking powder, salt, and baking soda into a large bowl. Cut in butter until mixture is crumbly. Add egg, orange peel, and orange juice all at once; stir just until mixture is evenly moist. Fold in raisins and cranberries.

Spoon into a greased 9 x 5 x 3-inch loaf pan. Bake at 350 degrees for 1 hour and 10 minutes, or until a toothpick inserted in center comes out clean. Remove from pan; cool on a wire rack.

If you choose, you may substitute cranberries for the raisins to have an all cranberry bread.

Recipe tested by the Food Department of *Parents' Magazine*

Lincoln's Cranberry-Apple Conserve

4 $\frac{1}{2}$ cups peeled, diced Winesap or other cooking apple

3 cups fresh cranberries

1 $\frac{1}{2}$ cups unsweetened apple juice

$\frac{1}{4}$ cup plus 2 tablespoons firmly packed brown sugar

$\frac{1}{4}$ cup golden raisins

2 teaspoons peeled, grated gingerroot

$\frac{1}{2}$ teaspoon ground cinnamon

1/8 teaspoon salt

1/8 teaspoon ground cloves

Combine all ingredients in a large saucepan; bring to a boil. Reduce heat to medium-low, and cook, uncovered, 10 minutes, stirring occasionally. Remove from heat; let cool. Serve chilled or at room temperature. Cover and store in refrigerator up to 1 week. Yield: 5 $\frac{1}{2}$ cups (about 12 calories per tablespoon).

This has been a family tradition in the Thompson house every year for the past 20 years.

Recipe found in the December 1991 *Cooking Light Magazine*

Kimberly's Candied Walnut Salad

mixed baby greens (spring mix—spinach, green romaine, red romaine, green
   leaf, baby red chard, baby green chard, baby oak leaf)
2 cups walnuts (can be bought candied or roasted plain with maple syrup
   and honey)
2 ounces goat cheese
1 cup dried cranberries

Candied walnuts can be made ahead of time but are best warm. To candy the
walnuts, cover the bottom of a fry pan with walnuts on medium-high heat.
Add 1 tablespoon of honey and 2 tablespoons of maple sugar. Mix nuts in the
pan until fully coated with a wooden spoon. Remove from heat and prepare
the rest of the salad.

Use as many greens as you can eat in one sitting. Place in a large bowl and add
cranberries. Crumble the goat cheese on top (can also be put into a bowl to be
added later at the table in case people do not like goat cheese). Sprinkle with
balsamic vinegar and olive oil. Add warm walnuts and serve!

We make this with our fresh garden greens! I have been making this salad for
guests at the Thompson house for many years.

Pigeon's Pretzels

Dijon mustard
fresh cranberries
pretzels

Crush the cranberries and mix with enough mustard to taste. Put in a bowl and serve with plenty of pretzels.

Try your hand at drawing your favorite landmark!

Write down some memories from your travels!

Make your own
Thanksgiving menu!

_____

_____

_____

_____

_____

_____

_____

_____

_____

_____

_____

_____

About the Author

Patapsco Valley State Park, Hollofield Area, Maryland. The park is forty miles from D.C., and fifteen miles from BWI in Baltimore.

Kimberly Thompson is an author and storyteller for children. Her favorite pastime is to travel with her children gathering research for new ideas. In addition to storytelling, she has her Masters of Arts in Curriculum Instruction and Design from Concordia University. Toulouse on the Loose is her first children's book. Ms. Thompson lives in the Chicagoland area with her husband and two daughters.

About the Illustrator

Chris Easey was born in Norfolk, England, more years ago than he cares to remember. Now he lives with his American partner Sharon in Illinois for six months of winter before returning to West Sussex, England, for six months of summer.

He taught high school geography for nearly 40 years in England and always enjoyed drawing and producing cartoons for colleagues whenever they left. Upon retiring, he was later given water colors and a sketchpad along with the words "do something"—and has been doing so ever since.

Order Info